IN THE TALL GRASS

IN THE TALL GRASS

A TERRIFYING STORY BY
STEPHEN KING
AND JOE HILL

Copyright © 2021 by Independent Bookstore Day Publishing

First (and only) Edition

Originally published by *Esquire* in 2012. The contents of this book remain the property of the authors or the original copyright holders. First Scribner ebook edition October 2012.

This book is a work of fiction. Names, characters, places, and incidents either are products of the author's imagination or are used fictitiously. Any resemblance to actual events or locales or persons, living or dead, is entirely coincidental.

Printed in the United States of America for Independent Bookstore Day

Book designer: Kristine Brogno

ISBN 978-1732970458

All rights reserved. No part of this book may be reproduced, scanned, or distributed in any form without permission.

Independent Bookstore Day Publishing
A program of the American Booksellers Association

www.indiebookstoreday.com

Independent Bookstore Day would like to thank the authors, Stephen King and Joe Hill, Chuck Verrill of Darhansoff & Verrill, and Rosalind Lippel at Scribner.

INTRODUCTION

I discovered "In the Tall Grass" on a flight from Miami to the annual BookExpo in New York City in 2012. I saw the name Joe Hill on a copy of *Esquire* crammed upside-down in the seat pocket in front of me. Turns out he'd co-authored a story with his father, Stephen King. Happening upon a collaboration between two of my favorite authors en route to the largest book gathering of the year felt like fate.

The story took me back to King's *Children of the Corn*, with remote asphalt cutting through nature on either side. Of course, the trip goes awry and, of course, nature hides something ancient and hungry. We get the sense that many people over decades, or even centuries, have found themselves in the same situation as our protagonists. We can only hope we're reading about these particular people at this particular moment because they are the heroes who will finally defeat evil.

As events in the tale turned from uneasy to frightening, the story stopped. I flipped through the magazine, looking for the rest of the story. In my excitement I neglected the fine print—this was only part one. When I got back to Miami, I subscribed to *Esquire* because I needed to read part two as soon as possible. I had to know whether the monster would be bested... or if it would feed.

AARON JOHN CURTIS, BOOKS & BOOKS, MIAMI, FLORIDA

IN THE TALL GRASS

He wanted quiet for a while instead of the radio, so you could say what happened was his fault. She wanted fresh air instead of the AC for a while, so you could say it was hers. But since they never would have heard the kid without both of those things, you'd really have to say it was a combination, which made it perfect Cal-and-Becky, because they had run in tandem all their lives. Cal and Becky DeMuth, born nineteen months apart. Their parents called them the Irish Twins.

"Becky picks up the phone and Cal says hello," Mr. DeMuth liked to say.

"Cal thinks party and Becky's already written out the guest list," Mrs. DeMuth liked to say.

Never a cross word between them, even when Becky, at the time a dorm-dwelling freshman, showed up at Cal's off-campus apartment one day to announce she was pregnant. Cal took it well. Their folks? Not quite so sanguine.

The off-campus apartment was in Durham, because Cal chose UNH. When Becky (at that point unpregnant, if not necessarily a virgin) made the same college choice two years later, you could have cut the lack of surprise and spread it on bread.

"At least he won't have to come home every damn weekend to hang out with her," Mrs. DeMuth said.

"Maybe we'll get some peace around here," Mr. DeMuth said. "After twenty years, give or take, all that togetherness gets a little tiresome."

Of course they didn't do everything together, because Cal sure as hell wasn't responsible for the bun in his sister's oven. And it had been solely Becky's idea to ask Uncle Jim and Aunt Anne if she could live with them for a while—just until the baby came. To the senior DeMuths, who were stunned and bemused by this turn of events, it seemed as reasonable a course as any. And when Cal suggested he also take the spring semester off so they could make the cross-country drive together, their folks didn't put up much of a fuss. They even agreed that Cal could stay with Becky in San Diego until the baby was born. Calvin might be able to find a little job and chip in on expenses.

"Pregnant at nineteen," Mrs. DeMuth said.

"You were pregnant at nineteen," Mr. DeMuth said.

"Yes, but I was mar-ried," Mrs. DeMuth pointed out.

"And to a damned nice fellow," Mr. DeMuth felt compelled to add.

Mrs. DeMuth sighed. "Becky will pick the first name and Cal will pick the second."

"Or vicey-versa," Mr. DeMuth said—also with a sigh. (Sometimes married couples are also Irish Twins.)

Becky's mother took Becky out for lunch one day not long before the kids left for the West Coast. "Are you sure you want to give the baby up for adoption?" she asked. "I know I don't have a right to ask, I'm only your mother, but your father is curious."

"I haven't entirely made up my mind," Becky said. "Cal will help me decide."

"What about the father, dear?"

Becky looked surprised. "Oh, he gets no say. He turned out to be a fool."

Mrs. DeMuth sighed.

• • •

So there they were in Kansas, on a warm spring day in April, riding in an eight-year-old Mazda with New Hampshire plates and a ghost of New England road salt still splashed on the rusty rocker panels. Quiet instead of the radio, open windows instead of the AC. As a result, both of them heard the voice. It was faint but clear.

"Help! Help! Somebody help me!"

Brother and sister exchanged startled looks. Cal, currently behind the wheel, pulled over immediately. Sand rattled against the undercarriage.

Before leaving Portsmouth they had decided they would steer clear of the turnpikes. Cal wanted to see the Kaskaskia Dragon in Vandalia, Illinois; Becky wanted to make her manners to the World's Largest Ball of Twine in Cawker City, Kansas (both missions accomplished); the pair of them felt they needed to hit Roswell and see some groovy extraterrestrial shit. Now they were well south of the Twine Ball—which had been hairy, and fragrant, and altogether more impressive than either of them had anticipated—out on a leg of Route 400. It was a well-maintained stretch of two-lane blacktop that would take them the rest of the way across the flat serving platter of Kansas to the Colorado line. Ahead of them were miles of road with nary a car or truck in sight. Ditto behind.

On their side of the highway there were a few houses, a boarded-up church called the Black Rock of the Redeemer (which Becky thought a queer name for a church, but this was Kansas), and a rotting Bowl-a-Drome that looked as if it might last have operated around the time the Trammps were committing pop-music arson by lighting a disco inferno. On the other side of 400 there was nothing but high green grass. It stretched all the way to a horizon that was both illimitable and unremarkable.

"Was that a—" Becky began. She was wearing a light coat unzipped over a midsection that was just beginning to bulge; she was well along into her sixth month.

He raised a hand without looking at her. He was looking at the grass. "Sh. Listen!"

They heard faint music coming from one of the houses. A dog gave a phlegmy triple bark—roop-roop-roop—and went still. Someone was hammering a board. And there was the steady, gentle susurration of the wind. Becky realized she could actually see the wind, combing the grass on the far side of the road. It made waves that ran away from them until they were lost in the distance.

Just when Cal was beginning to think they hadn't, after all, heard anything—it wouldn't be the first time they had imagined something together—the cry came again.

"Help! Please help me!" And: "I'm lost!"

This time the look they exchanged was full of alarmed understanding. The grass was incredibly tall. (For such an expanse of grass to be over six feet high this early in the season was an anomaly that wouldn't occur to them until later.) Some little kid had wandered into it, probably while exploring, almost certainly from one of the houses down the road. He had become disoriented and wandered in even deeper. He sounded about eight, which would make him far too short to leap up and find his bearings that way.

"We should haul him out," Cal said.

"Yep. Little rescue mission. Pull into the church parking lot. Let's get off the side of the road."

He left her on the margin of the highway and turned into the dirt lot of the Redeemer. A scattering of dust-filmed cars was parked here, windshields beetle bright in the glare of the sun. That all but one of these cars appeared to have been there for days—even weeks—was another anomaly that would not strike them until later.

While he took care of the car, Becky crossed to the other shoulder.

She cupped her hands to her mouth and shouted. "Kid! Hey, kid! Can you hear me?"

After a moment he called back: "Yes! Help me! I've been in here for DAYS!"

Becky, who remembered how little kids judged time, guessed that might mean twenty minutes or so. She looked for a path of broken or trampled grass where the kid had gone in (probably making up some video game or stupid jungle movie in his head as he did), and couldn't see one. But that was all right; she pegged the voice as coming from her left, at about ten o'clock. Not too far in, either. Which made sense; if he'd gotten in very far, they wouldn't have heard him even with the radio off and the windows open.

She was about to descend the embankment to the edge of the grass, when there came a second voice, a woman's—hoarse and confused. She had the groggy rasp of someone who has just come awake and needs a drink of water. Badly.

"Don't!" shouted the woman. "Don't! Please! Stay away! Tobin, stop calling! Stop making noise, honey! He'll hear you!"

"Hello?" Becky yelled. "What's going on?"

Behind her, she heard a door slam. Cal, on his way across the street.

"We're lost!" the boy shouted. "Please! Please, my mom is hurt, please! Please help!"

"No!" the woman said. "No, Tobin, no!"

Becky looked around to see what was taking Cal so long.

He had crossed a few dozen feet of the dirt parking lot and then hesitated by what looked like a first-generation Prius. It was filmed with a pale coat of road dust, almost completely obscuring the windshield. Cal hunched slightly, shielded his eyes with one hand, and squinted through the side window at something in the passenger seat. Frowning to himself for a moment, and then flinching, as if from a horsefly.

"Please!" the boy said. "We're lost and I can't find the road!"

"Tobin!" the woman started to call, but then her voice choked. As if she didn't have the spit for talk.

Unless this was an elaborate prank, something was very wrong here. Becky DeMuth was not conscious of her hand drifting to press against the tight, beach-ball-firm curve of her abdomen. Nor did she connect the way she felt then with the dreams that had been bothering her for close to two months now, dreams she had not discussed even with Cal—the ones about driving at night. A child shouted in those dreams, too.

She dropped down the embankment in two long-legged steps. It was steeper than it looked, and when she reached the bottom, it was clear the grass was even higher than she thought, closer to seven feet than six.

The breeze gusted. The wall of grass surged and retreated in a soft shushing tide.

"Don't look for us!" the woman called.

"Help!" said the boy, contradicting her, almost shouting over her—and his voice was close. Becky could hear him just off to the left. Not close enough to reach in and grab, but surely no more than ten or twelve yards from the road.

"I'm over here, buddy," she called to him. "Keep walking toward me.

You're almost to the road. You're almost out."

"Help! Help! I still can't find you!" the boy said, his voice even closer now. This was followed by a hysterical, sobbing laugh that cooled Becky's skin.

Cal took a single skipping step down the embankment, slid on his heels, and almost fell on his ass. The ground was wet. If Becky hesitated to wade into the thick grass and go get the boy, it was because she didn't want to soak her shorts. Grass that high would hold enough water, suspended in glittering drops, to make a small pond.

"Why are you waiting?" Cal asked.

"There's a woman with him," Becky said. "She's being weird."

"Where are you?" the boy cried, almost babbled, from just a few feet away in the grass. Becky looked for a flash of his pants or shirt, but didn't see them. He was just a little bit too far in for that. "Are you coming? Please! I can't find my way out!"

"Tobin!" the mother yelled, her voice distant and strained. "Tobin, stop!"

"Hang on," Cal said, and stepped into the grass. "Captain Cal, to the rescue. Have no fear. When kids see me, they want to be me."

By then, Becky had her cell phone out, cupped in one hand, and was opening her mouth to ask Cal if they should call highway patrol or whatever they had out here that was blue.

Cal took one step, then another, and suddenly all Becky could see of him was the back of his denim shirt, and his khaki shorts. For no rational reason at all, the thought of him moving out of sight caused her pulse to jump.

Still, she glanced at the face of her little black touchscreen Android and saw that she had the full complement of five bars. She dialed 9-1-1, and hit Call. As she lifted the phone to her ear, she took a long step into the grass.

The phone rang once, then a robot voice announced that her call was being recorded. Becky took another step, not wanting to lose sight of the blue shirt and light-brown shorts. Cal was always so impatient. Of course, so was she.

Wet grass began to whicker against her blouse, shorts, and bare legs. From the bathing machine came a din, Becky thought, her subconscious coughing up part of a half-digested limerick, one of Edward Gorey's. As of jollification within. It was heard far and wide and the something something tide blah blah. She had written a paper on limericks for her Freshman Lit class that she had thought was rather clever, but all she got for her trouble was a headful of dumb rhymes she couldn't forget, and a C+.

A real live lady-voice supplanted the robot. "Kiowa County 9-1-1, what is your location and the nature of your emergency, caller?"

"I'm on Route 400," Becky said. "I don't know the name of the town, but there's some church, the Rock of the Redeemer or something . . . and this broken-down old roller-skating rink . . . no, I guess it's a bowling alley . . . and some kid is lost in the grass. His mother, too. We hear them calling. The kid's close, the mother not so much. The kid sounds scared, the mother just sounds—" Weird, she meant to finish, but didn't get the chance.

"Caller, we've got a very bad connection here. Please restate your—"

Then nothing. Becky stopped to look at her phone and saw a single bar. While she was watching, it disappeared, to be replaced by NO SERVICE. When she looked up, her brother had been swallowed by the green.

Overhead, a jet traced a white contrail across the sky at thirty-five thousand feet.

• • •

"Help! Help me!"

The kid was close, but maybe not quite as close as Cal had thought. And a little farther to the left.

"Go back to the road!" the woman screamed. Now she sounded closer, too. "Go back while you still can!"

"Mom! Mommy! They want to HELP!"

Then the kid just screamed. It rose to an ear-stabbing shriek, wavered, suddenly turned into more hysterical laughter. There were thrashing sounds—maybe panic, maybe the sounds of a struggle. Cal bolted in that direction, sure he was going to burst into some beaten-down clearing and discover the kid—Tobin—and his mother being assaulted by a knife-wielding maniac out of a Quentin Tarantino movie. He got ten yards and was just realizing that had to be too far when the grass snarled around his left ankle. He grabbed at more grass on his way down and did nothing but tear out a double handful that drooled sticky green juice down his palms to his wrists. He fell full-length on the oozy ground and managed to snork mud up both nostrils. Marvelous. How come there was never a tree around when you needed one?

He got to his knees. "Kid? Tobin? Sing—" He sneezed mud, wiped his face, and now smelled grass-goo when he inhaled. Better and better. A true sensory bouquet. "Sing out! You too, Mom!"

Mom didn't. Tobin did.

"Help me pleeease!"

Now the kid was on Cal's right, and he sounded quite a lot deeper in the grass than before. How could that be? He sounded close enough to grab.

Cal turned around, expecting to see his sister, but there was only grass. Tall grass. It should have been broken down where he ran through it, but it wasn't. There was only the smashed-flat place where he'd gone full length, and even there the greenery was already springing back up. Tough grass they had here in Kansas. Tough tall grass.

"Becky? Beck?"

"Chill, I'm right here," she said, and although he couldn't see her, he would in a second; she was practically on top of him. She sounded disgusted. "I lost the 9-1-1 chick."

"That's okay, just don't lose me." He turned in the other direction, and cupped his hands to his mouth. "Tobin!"

Nothing.

"Tobin!"

"What?" Faint. Jesus Christ, what was the kid doing? Lighting out for Nebraska? "Are you coming? You have to keep coming! I can't find you!"

"KID, STAND STILL!" Shouting so loud and so hard it hurt his vocal cords. It was like being at a Metallica concert, only without the music. "I DON'T CARE HOW SCARED YOU ARE, STAND STILL! LET US COME TO YOU!"

He turned around, once more expecting to see Becky, but he only saw the grass. He flexed his knees and jumped. He could see the road (farther away than he expected; he must have run quite some way without realizing it). He could see the church—Holy Hank's House of Hallelujah, or whatever it was called—and he could see the Bowl-a-Drome, but that was all. He didn't really expect to see Becky's head, she was only five-two, but he did expect to see her route of passage through the grass. Only the wind was combing through it harder than ever, and that made it seem like there were dozens of possible paths.

He jumped again. Soggy ground squashed each time he came down. Those little licking peeks back at Highway 400 were maddening.

"Becky? Where the hell are you?"

• • •

Becky heard Cal bellow for the kid to stand still no matter how scared he was, and let them come to him. Which sounded like a good plan, if only her idiot brother would let her catch up. She was winded, she was wet, and she was for the first time feeling truly pregnant. The good news was that Cal was close, on her right at one o'clock.

Fine, but my sneakers are going to be ruined. In fact, the Beckster believes they're ruined already.

"Becky? Where the hell are you?"

Okay, this was strange. He was still on her right, but now he sounded closer to five o'clock. Like, almost behind her.

"Here," she said. "And I'm going to stay here until you get to me." She glanced down at her Android. "Cal, do you have any bars on your phone?"

"I don't have any idea. It's in the car. Just keep yakking until I get to you."

"What about the kid? And the crazy mom? She's gone totally dark."

"Let's get back together—then we'll worry about them, okay?" he said. Becky knew her brother, and she didn't like the way he sounded. This was Cal being worried and trying not to show it. "For now, just talk to me."

Becky considered, then began to recite, stamping her muddy sneakers in time. "There once was a guy named McSweeney, who spilled some gin on his weenie. Just to be couth he added vermouth, then slipped his girl a martini."

"Oh, that's charming," he said. Now directly behind her, almost close enough to reach out and touch, and why was that such a relief? It was only a field, for God's sake.

"Hey, you guys!" The kid. Faint. Not laughing now, just sounding lost and terrified. "Are you looking for me? You there, Captain Cal? I'm scared!"

"YES! YES, OKAY! HANG ON," her brother hollered. "Becky? Becky, keep talking."

Becky's hands went to her bulge—she refused to call it a baby-bump, that was so People magazine—and cradled it lightly. "Here's another.

There once was a woman named Jill, who swallowed an exploding pi—"

"Stop, stop. I overshot you somehow."

Yup, his voice was now coming from ahead. She turned around again. "Quit goofing, Cal. This is not funny." Her mouth was dry. She swallowed, and her throat was dry, too. When it made that click sound, you knew you were dry. There was a big bottle of Poland Spring water in the car. Also a couple of Cokes in the backseat. She could see them: red cans, white letters.

"Becky?"

"What?"

"There's something wrong here."

"What do you mean?" Thinking: As if I didn't know.

"Listen to me. Can you jump?"

"Of course I can jump! What do you think?"

"I think you're going to have a baby this summer, that's what I think."

"I can still . . . Cal, stop walking away!"

"I didn't move," he said.

"You did, you must have! You still are!"

"Shut up and listen. I'm going to count to three. On three, you put your hands over your head like a ref signaling the field goal's good and jump just as high as you can. I'll do the same. You won't need to get much air for me to see your hands, 'kay? And I'll come to you."

Oh whistle and I'll come to you, my lad, she thought—no idea where it had come from, something else from Freshman Lit maybe, but one thing she did know was that he could say he wasn't moving but he was, he was getting farther away all the time.

"Becky? Beck—"

"All right!" she screamed. "All right, let's do it!"

"One! Two!—" he cried. "THREE!"

At fifteen, Becky DeMuth had weighed eighty-two pounds—her father called her Stick—and ran hurdles with the varsity team. At fifteen, she could walk from one end of the school to the other on her hands. She wanted to believe she was still that person; some part of her had honestly expected to remain that person for her entire life. Her mind had still not caught up to being nineteen and pregnant . . . not eighty-two pounds but one hundred thirty. She wanted to grab air—Houston, we have liftoff—but it was like trying to jump while giving a small child a piggyback. (When you thought about it, that was pretty much the case.)

Her eyeline only cleared the top of the grass for a moment, affording her the briefest glimpse back the way she had come. What she saw, though, was enough to make her almost breathless with alarm.

Cal and the road. Cal . . . and the road.

She came back down, felt a shock of impact jolt up through her heels and into her knees. The squodgy ground under her left foot melted away. She dropped and sat down in the rich black muck with another jolt of impact, a literal whack in the ass.

Becky thought she had walked twenty steps into the grass. Maybe thirty at most. The road should've been close enough to hit with a Frisbee. It was, instead, as if she had walked the length of a football field and then some. A battered red Datsun, zipping along the highway, looked no bigger than a Matchbox car. A hundred and forty yards of grass—a softly flowing ocean of watered green silk—stood between her and that slender blacktop thread.

Her first thought, sitting in the mud, was: No. Impossible. You didn't see what you think you saw.

Her second thought was of a weak swimmer, caught in a retreating tide, pulled farther and farther from shore, not understanding how much trouble she was in until she began to scream and discovered no one on the beach could hear her.

As shaken as she was by the sight of the improbably distant highway, her brief glimpse of Cal was just as disorienting. Not because he was far away, but because he was really close. She had seen him spring up above the grass less than ten feet away, but the two of them had been screaming for all they were worth just to make themselves heard.

The muck was warm, sticky, placental.

The grass hummed furiously with insects.

"Be careful!" the boy shouted. "Don't you get lost too!"

This was followed by another brief burst of laughter—a giddy, nervous sob of hilarity. It wasn't Cal, and it wasn't the kid, not this time. It wasn't the woman, either. This laughter came from somewhere to her left, then died out, swallowed by bug song. It was male and had a quality of drunkenness to it.

Becky suddenly remembered one of the things Weirdo Mom had shouted: Stop calling, honey! He'll hear you!

What the fuck?

"What the FUCK?" shouted Cal. She wasn't surprised. Ike and Mike, they think alike, Mrs. DeMuth liked to say. Frick and Frack, got two heads but just one back, Mr. DeMuth liked to say.

A pause in which there was only the sound of the wind and the reeeee of the bugs. Then, bellowing at the top of his lungs: "What the fuck IS this?"

• • •

Cal had a brief period, about five minutes later, when he lost it a little. It happened after he tried an experiment. He jumped and looked at the road and landed and waited and then after he had counted to thirty, he jumped and looked again.

If you wanted to be a stickler for accuracy, you could say he was already losing it a little to even think he needed to try such an experiment. But by then reality was starting to feel much like the ground underfoot: liquid and treacherous. He could not manage the simple trick of walking toward his sister's voice, which came from the right when he was walking left, and from the left when he was walking right. Sometimes from ahead and sometimes from behind. And no matter which direction he walked in, he seemed to move farther from the road.

He jumped and fixed his gaze on the steeple of the church. It was a brilliant white spear set against the background of that bright blue, almost cloudless sky. Crappy church, divine, soaring steeple. The congregation must have paid through the nose for that baby, he thought. Although from here—maybe a quarter of a mile off, and never mind that was crazy, he had walked less than a hundred feet—

he could not see the peeling paint, or the boards in the windows. He couldn't even make out his own car, tucked in with the other distance-shrunken cars in the lot. He could, however, see the dusty Prius. That one was in the front row. He was trying not to dwell on what he had glimpsed in the passenger seat . . . a bad-dream detail that he wasn't ready to examine just yet.

On that first jump, he was turned to face the steeple dead-on, and in any normal world, he should've been able to reach it by walking through the grass in a straight line, jumping every now and then to make minor course corrections. There was a rusting, bullet-peppered sign between the church and the bowling alley, diamond-shaped with a yellow border: SLOW CHILDREN X-ING, maybe. He couldn't be sure—he had left his glasses in the car, too.

He dropped back down into the squidgy muck and began to count.

"Cal?" came his sister's voice from somewhere behind him.

"Wait," he shouted.

"Cal?" she said again, from somewhere to his left. "Do you want me to keep talking?" And when he didn't reply, she began to chant in a desultory voice, from somewhere in front of him: "There once was a girl went to Yale . . ."

"Just shut up and wait!" he screamed again.

His throat felt dry and tight and swallowing took an effort. Although it was close to two in the afternoon, the sun seemed to hover almost directly overhead. He could feel it on his scalp, and the tops of his ears, which were tender, beginning to burn. He thought if he could just have something to drink—a cold swallow of spring water, or one of their Cokes—he might not feel so frayed, so anxious.

Drops of dew burned in the grass, a hundred miniature magnifying glasses refracting and intensifying the light.

Ten seconds.

"Kid?" Becky called, from somewhere on his right. (No. Stop. She's not moving. Get your head under control.) She sounded thirsty, too. Croaky. "Are you still with us?"

"Yes! Did you find my mom?"

"Not yet!" Cal shouted, thinking it really had been a while since they had heard from her. Not that she was his main concern just then.

Twenty seconds.

"Kid?" Becky said. Her voice came from behind him again. "Everything's going to be all right."

"Have you seen my dad?"

Cal thought: A new player. Terrific. Maybe William Shatner's in here, too. Also Mike Huckabee . . . Kim Kardashian . . . the guy who plays Opie on Sons of Anarchy and the entire cast of The Walking Dead.

He closed his eyes, but the moment he did he felt dizzy, as if he were standing on the top of a ladder beginning to sway underfoot. He wished he hadn't thought of The Walking Dead. He should have stuck with William Shatner and Marvelous Mike Huckabee. He opened his eyes again, and found himself rocking on his heels. He steadied himself with some effort. The heat made his face prickle with sweat.

Thirty. He had been standing in this one spot for thirty seconds. He thought he should wait a full minute, but couldn't, and so he jumped for another look back at the church.

A part of him—a part he had been trying with all his will to ignore—already knew what he was going to see. This part had been providing an almost jovial running commentary: Everything will have moved, Cal, good buddy. The grass flows and you flow too. Think of it as becoming one with nature, bro.

When his tired legs lofted him into the air again, he saw the church steeple was now off to his left. Not a lot—just a little. But he had drifted far enough to his right that he was no longer seeing the front of that diamond-shaped sign, but the silver aluminum back of it. Also, he wasn't sure, but he thought it was all just a little farther away than it had been. As if he had backed up a few steps while he was counting to thirty.

Somewhere, the dog barked again: roop, roop. Somewhere a radio was playing. He couldn't make out the song, just the thump of the bass. The insects thrummed their single lunatic note.

"Oh, come on," Cal said. He had never been much for talking to himself—as an adolescent, he had cultivated a Buddhist skateboarder vibe, and had prided himself on how long he could serenely maintain his silence—but he was talking now, and hardly aware of it. "Oh, come the fuck on. This is . . . this is nuts."

He was walking, too. Walking for the road—again, almost without knowing it.

"Cal?" Becky shouted.

"This is just nuts," he said again, breathing hard, shoving at the grass. His foot caught on something, and he went down knee-first into an inch of swampy water. Hot water—not lukewarm, hot, as hot as bathwater—splashed up onto the crotch of his shorts, providing him with the sensation of having just pissed himself.

That broke him a little. He lunged back to his feet. Running now. Grass whipping at his face. It was sharp-edged and tough, and when one green sword snapped him under the left eye, he felt it, a sharp stinging. The pain gave him a nasty jump, and he ran harder, going as fast as he could now.

"Help me!" the kid screamed, and how about this? *Help* came from Cal's left, *me* from his right. It was the Kansas version of Dolby Stereo.

"This is nuts!" Cal screamed again. "This is nuts, it's nuts, it's FUCKING nuts!" The words running together, *itsnutsitsnuts*, what a stupid thing to say, what an inane observation, and he couldn't stop saying it.

He fell again, hard this time, sprawling chest-first. By now his clothes were spattered with earth so rich, warm, and dark, it felt and even smelled like fecal matter.

Cal picked himself back up, ran another five steps, felt grass snarl around his legs—it was like putting his feet into a nest of tangling wire—and goddamn if he didn't fall a third time. The inside of his head buzzed, like a cloud of bluebottles.

"Cal!" Becky was screaming. "Cal, stop! Stop!"

Yes, stop. If you don't you'll be yelling "Help me" right along with the kid. A fucking duet.

He gulped at the air. His heart galloped. He waited for the buzzing in his head to pass, then realized it wasn't in his head after all. They really were flies. He could see them shooting in and out through the grass, a swarm of them around something through the shifting curtain of yellow-green, just ahead of him.

He pushed his hands into the grass and parted it to see.

A dog—it looked like it had been a golden retriever—was on its side in the mire. Limp brownish-red fur glittered beneath a shifting mat of flies. Its bloated tongue lolled between its gums, and the cloudy marbles of its eyes strained from its head. The rusting tag of its collar gleamed deep in its fur. Cal looked again at the tongue. It was coated a greenish-white. Cal didn't want to think why. The dog's dirty coat looked like a filthy yellow carpet tossed on a heap of bones. Some of that fur drifted—little fluffs of it—on the warm breeze.

Take hold. It was his thought, but in his father's steadying voice. Making that voice helped. He stared at the dog's caved-in stomach and saw lively movement there. A boiling stew of maggots. Like the ones he'd seen squirming on the half-eaten hamburgers lying on the passenger seat of that damned Prius. Burgers that had been there for days. Someone had left them, walked away from the car and left them, and never come back, and never—

Take hold, Calvin. If not for yourself, for your sister.

"I will," he promised his father. "I will."

He stripped the snarls of tough greenery from his ankles and shins, barely feeling the little cuts the grass had inflicted. He stood.

"Becky, where are you?"

Nothing for a long time—long enough for his heart to abandon his chest and rise into his throat. Then, incredibly distant: "Here! Cal, what should we do? We're lost!"

He closed his eyes again, briefly. That's the kid's line. Then he thought: Le kid, c'est moi. It was almost funny.

"We keep calling," he said, moving toward where her voice had come from. "We keep calling until we're together again."

"But I'm so thirsty!" She sounded closer now, but Cal didn't trust that. No, no, no.

"Me too," he said. "But we're going to get out of this, Beck. We just have to keep our heads." That he had already lost his—a little, only a little—was one thing he'd never tell her. She had never told him the name of the boy who knocked her up, after all, and that made them sort of even. A secret for her, now one for him.

"What about the kid?"

Ah, Christ, now she was fading again. He was so scared that the truth popped out with absolutely no trouble at all, and at top volume.

"Fuck the kid, Becky! This is about us now!"

• • •

Directions melted in the tall grass, and time melted as well: a Dalí world with Kansas stereo. They chased each other's voices like weary children too stubborn to give up their game of tag and come in for dinner. Sometimes Becky sounded close; sometimes she sounded far; he never once saw her. Occasionally the kid yelled for someone to help him, once so close that Cal sprang into the grass with his hands outstretched to snare him before he could get away, but there was no kid. Only a crow with its head and one wing torn off.

There is no morning or night here, Cal thought, only eternal afternoon. But even as this idea occurred to him, he saw that the blue of the sky was deepening and the squelchy ground beneath his sodden feet was growing dim.

If we had shadows, they'd be getting long and we might use them to move in the same direction, at least, he thought, but they had no shadows. Not in the tall grass. He looked at his watch and wasn't surprised to see it had stopped even though it was a self-winder. The grass had stopped it. He felt sure of it. Some malignant vibe in the grass; some paranormal Fringe shit.

It was half past nothing when Becky began to sob.

"Beck? Beck?"

"I have to rest, Cal. I have to sit down. I'm so thirsty. And I've been having cramps."

"Contractions?"

"I guess so. Oh God, what if I have a miscarriage out here in this fucking field?"

"Just sit where you are," he said. "They'll pass."

"Thanks, doc, I'll—" Nothing. Then she began screaming. "Get away from me! Get away! DON'T TOUCH ME!"

Cal, now too tired to run, ran anyway.

• • •

Even in her shock and terror, Becky knew who the madman had to be when he brushed aside the grass and stood before her. He was wearing tourist clothes—Dockers and mud-clotted Bass Weejuns. The real giveaway, however, was his T-shirt. Although smeared with mud and a dark maroon crust that was almost certainly blood, she could see the ball of spaghetti-like string and knew what was printed above it—world's largest ball of twine, cawker city, kansas. Didn't she have a shirt just like it neatly folded in her suitcase?

The kid's dad. In the mud- and grass-smeared flesh.

"Get away from me!" She leaped to her feet, hands cradling her belly. "Get away! DON'T TOUCH ME!"

Dad grinned. His cheeks were stubbly, his lips red. "Calm down. Want to get out? It's easy."

She stared at him, openmouthed. Cal was shouting, but for the moment she paid no attention.

"If you could get out," she said, "you wouldn't still be in."

He tittered. "Right idea. Wrong conclusion. I was just going to hook up with my boy. Already found my wife. Want to meet her?"

She said nothing.

"Okay, be that way," he said, and turned from her. He started into the grass. Soon he would melt away, just as her brother had, and Becky felt a stab of panic. He was clearly mad, you only had to look into his eyes or listen to his text-message vocal delivery to know that, but he was human.

He stopped and turned back, grinning. "Forgot to introduce myself. My bad. Ross Humbolt's the name. Real estate's the game.

Poughkeepsie. Wife's Natalie. Little boy's Tobin. Sweet kid! Smart! You're Becky. Brother's Cal. Last chance, Becky. Come with me or die." His eyes dropped to her belly. "Baby, too."

Don't trust him.

She didn't, but followed just the same. At what she hoped was a safe distance. "You have no idea where you're going."

"Becky? Becky!" Cal. But far away. Somewhere in North Dakota. Maybe Manitoba. She supposed she should answer him, but her throat was too raw.

"I was just as lost in the grass as you two," he said. "Not anymore. Kissed the stone." He turned briefly and regarded her with roguish, mad eyes. "Hugged it, too. Whsssh. See it then. All those little dancing fellas. See everything. Clear as day. Back to the road? Straight shot! If I'm line I'm dine. Wife's right up here. You have to meet her. She's my honey. Makes the best martini in America. There once was a guy named McSweeney, who spilled some gin on his ahem! Just to be couth, he added vermouth. I guess you know the rest." He winked at her.

In high school, Becky had taken a gym elective called Self-Defense for Young Women. Now she tried to remember the moves, and couldn't. The only thing she could remember . . .

Deep in the right pocket of her shorts was a key ring. The longest and thickest key fit the front door of the house where she and her brother had grown up. She separated it from the others and pressed it between the first two fingers of her hand.

"Here she is!" Ross Humbolt proclaimed jovially, parting high grass with both hands, like an explorer in some old movie. "Say hello,

Natalie! This young woman is going to have a critter!"

There was blood splashed on the grass beyond the swatches he was holding open and Becky wanted to stop but her feet carried her forward and he even stepped aside a little like in one of those other old movies where the suave guy says After you doll and they enter the swanky nightclub where the jazz combo's playing only this was no swanky nightclub this was a beaten-down swatch of grass where the woman Natalie Humbolt if that was her name was lying all twisted with her eyes bulging and her dress pushed up to show great big red divots in her thighs and Becky guessed she knew now why Ross Humbolt of Poughkeepsie had such red lips and one of Natalie's arms was torn off at the shoulder and lying ten feet beyond her in crushed grass already springing back up and there were more great big red divots in the arm and the red was still wet because... because...

Because she hasn't been dead that long, Becky thought. We heard her scream. We heard her die.

"Family's been here awhile," Ross Humbolt said in a chummy, confidential tone as his grass-stained fingers settled around Becky's throat. He hiccuped. "Folks can get pretty hungry. No Mickey D's out here! Nope. You can drink the water that comes out of the ground—it's gritty and awful damn warm, but after a while you don't mind that— only we've been in here for days. I'm full now, though. Full as a tick." His bloodstained lips descended into the cup of her ear, and his beard stubble tickled her skin as he whispered. "Want to see the rock? Want to lay on it naked, and feel me in you, beneath the pinwheel stars, while the grass sings our names? Poetry, eh?"

She tried to suck a chestful of air to scream, but nothing came down her windpipe. In her lungs was a sudden, dreadful vacancy. He screwed his thumbs into her throat, crushing muscle, tendon, soft tissue. Ross Humbolt grinned. His teeth were stained red, but his tongue was a yellowish-green. His breath smelled of blood; also like a fresh-clipped lawn.

"The grass has things to tell you. You just need to learn to listen. You need to learn how to speak Tall Weed, honey. The rock knows. After you see the rock you'll understand. I've learned more from that rock in two days than I learned in twenty years of schooling."

He had her bent backward, her spine arched. She bent like a high blade of grass in the wind. His green breath gushed in her face again.

"Twenty years of schooling and they put me on the gray shift," he said, and laughed. "That's some good old rock, isn't it? Dylan. Child of Yahweh. Bard of Hibbing and I ain't ribbing. I'll tell you what. The stone in the center of this field is a good old rock, but it's a thirsty rock. It's been working on the gray shift since before red men hunted on the Osage Cuestas, been working since a glacier brought it here during the last Ice Age, and oh girl, it's so fucking thirsty."

She wanted to drive her knee into his balls, but it was all too much effort. The best she could do was lift her foot a few inches and then gently set it down again. Lift the foot and set it down. Lift and set. She seemed to be stamping her heel in slow motion, like a horse ready to be let out of a stall.

Constellations of black and silver sparks exploded at the edges of her vision. Pinwheel stars, she thought. It was oddly fascinating, watching as new universes were born and died, appearing and winking out. She would soon be winking out herself, she understood. This did not seem such a terrible thing. Urgent action was not required.

Cal was screaming her name from very far away. If he had been in Manitoba before, now he was down a mine shaft in Manitoba.

Her hand tightened on the key ring in her pocket. The teeth of some of those keys were digging into her palm. Biting.

"Blood is nice, tears are better," Ross said. "For a thirsty old rock like that. And when I fuck you on the stone, it'll have some of both. Has to be quick, though. Don't want to do it in front of the kid. We're Baptists." His breath stank.

She pulled her hand out of her pocket, the end of her house key protruding between her pointer and middle finger, and jabbed her fist into Ross Humbolt's face. She just wanted to push his mouth away, didn't want him breathing on her, didn't want to smell the green stink of him anymore. Her arm felt weak, and the way she punched at him was lazy, almost friendly—but the key caught him under the left eye, and raked down his cheek, sketching a jaggedy line in blood.

He flinched, snapping his head back. His hands loosened; for an instant his thumbs were no longer burrowing into the soft skin in the hollow of her throat. A moment later he tightened his grip again, but by then she had drawn a single whooping breath. The sparks—the pinwheel stars—bursting and flaring at the periphery of her vision faded out. Her head went clear, as clear as if someone had dashed icy water into her face. The next time she punched him, she put her shoulder behind it, and sank the key into his eye. Her knuckles jarred against bone. The key popped through his cornea and into the liquid center of the eyeball.

He did not scream. He made a kind of doglike bark, a woofing grunt, and wrenched her hard to one side, trying to yank her off her feet. His forearms were sunburnt and peeling. Close up she could see his nose was peeling too, badly, the bridge of his nose sizzling with sunburn. He grimaced, showing teeth stained pink and green.

Her hand fell away, let go of the key ring. It continued to dangle from the welling socket of his left eye, the other keys dancing against each other and bouncing against his stubbly cheek. Blood slicked the entire left side of Humbolt's face, and that eye was a glimmering red hole.

The grass seethed around them. The wind rose, and the tall blades thrashed and flailed at Becky's back and legs.

He kneed her in the belly. It was like being clubbed with a piece of stovewood. Becky felt pain and something worse than pain, in a low place where abdomen met groin. It was a kind of muscular contraction, a twisting, as if there were a knotted rope in her womb, and someone had just yanked it tight; tighter than it was supposed to go.

"Oh Becky! Oh girl! Your ass—your ass is grass now!" he screamed, a note of mad hilarity wavering in his voice.

He kneed her in the stomach again and then a third time. Each blow set off a fresh, black, poisonous detonation. He's killing the baby, Becky thought. Something trickled down the inside of her left leg. Whether it was blood or urine, she could not have said.

They danced together, the pregnant woman and the one-eyed

madman. They danced in the grass, feet squelching, his hands on her throat. The two of them had staggered in a wavering semicircle around the corpse of Natalie Humbolt. Becky was aware of the dead body to her left, had glimpses of pale, bloody, bitten thighs, rumpled jean skirt, and Natalie's exposed grass-stained granny panties. And her arm—Natalie's arm in the grass, just behind Ross Humbolt's feet. Natalie's dirty, severed arm (how had he removed it? had he torn it off like a chicken drumstick?) lay with fingers slightly curled, filth under her cracked fingernails.

Becky threw herself at Ross, heaved her weight forward. He stepped back, put his foot on that arm, and it turned beneath his heel. He made an angry, grunting cry of distress as he spilled over, pulling her with him. He did not let go of her throat until he hit the ground, his teeth coming together with an audible clack!

He absorbed most of the impact, the springy mass of his suburban-Baptist gut softening her own fall. She shoved herself off him, began to scramble on all fours into the grass.

Only she couldn't move quickly. Her insides pulsed with a dreadful weight and feeling of tension, as if she had swallowed a medicine ball. She wanted to vomit.

He caught her ankle and pulled. She fell flat, onto her hurt, throbbing stomach. A lance of rupturing pain went through her abdomen, a feeling of something bursting. Her chin struck the wet earth. Her vision swarmed with black specks.

"Where are you going, Becky DeMuth?" She had not told him her last name. He couldn't know that. "I'll just find you again. The grass will show me where you're hiding, the little dancing men will take me right to you. Come here. You don't need to go to San Diego now. No decisions about the baby will be necessary. All done now."

Her vision cleared. She saw, right in front of her, on a flattened bit of grass, a woman's straw purse, the contents dumped out, and amid the mess, a little pair of manicuring scissors—they almost looked more like pliers than scissors. The blades were gummy with blood. She didn't want to think how Ross Humbolt of Poughkeepsie might have used that tool, or how she herself might now use it.

Nevertheless, she closed her hand around it.

"Come here, I said," Ross told her. "Now, bitch." Hauling on her foot.

She twisted and shoved herself back at him, with Natalie Humbolt's manicure scissors in one fist. She struck him in the face, once, twice, three times, before he began to scream. It was a scream of pain, even if, before she was done with him, it had turned into great, sobbing guffaws of laughter. She thought: The kid laughed, too. Then for quite a while she thought nothing. Not until after moonrise.

• • •

In the last of the day's light, Cal sat in the grass, brushing tears off his cheeks.

He never gave way to full-on weeping. He only dropped onto his butt, after who knew how much fruitless wandering and calling for Becky—she had long since stopped replying to him—and then for a while his eyes were tingling and damp, and his breath a little thick.

Dusk was glorious. The sky was a deep, austere blue, darkening almost to black, and in the west, behind the church, the horizon was lit with the infernal glow of dying coals. He saw it now and then, when he had the energy to jump and look, and could persuade himself there was some point in looking around.

His sneakers were soaked through, which made them heavy, and his feet ached. The insides of his thighs itched. He took off his right shoe, and dumped a dingy trickle of water from it. He wasn't wearing socks, and his bare foot had the ghastly white, shriveled look of a drowned thing.

He removed the other sneaker, was about to dump it, then hesitated. He brought it to his lips, tipped back his head, and let gritty water—water that tasted like his own stinking foot—run over his tongue.

He had heard Becky and the Man, a long way off in the grass. Had heard the Man speaking to her in a gleeful, inebriated voice, lecturing her almost, although Cal had not been able to make out much of what was actually said. Something about a rock. Something about dancing men. Something about being thirsty. A line from some old folk song. What had the guy been singing? Twenty years of writing and they put you on the night shift. No—that wasn't right. But something close to that. Folk music wasn't an area of expertise for Cal; he was more of a Rush fan. They had been surfing on Permanent Waves all the way across the country.

Then he heard the two of them thrashing and struggling in the grass, heard Becky's choked cries, and the man ranting at her. Finally there came screams . . . screams that were terribly like shouts of hilarity. Not Becky. The Man.

By that point Cal had been hysterical, running and jumping and screaming for her. He shouted and ran for a long time before he finally got himself under control, forced himself to stop and listen. He had bent over, clutching his knees and panting, his throat achy with thirst, and had turned his attention to the silence.

The grass hushed.

"Becky?" he had called again, in a hoarsened voice. "Beck?"

No reply except for the wind slithering in the weeds.

He walked a little more. He called again. He sat. He tried not to cry.

And dusk was glorious.

He searched his pockets, for the hundredth hopeless time, gripped by the terrible fantasy of discovering a dry, linty stick of Juicy Fruit. He had bought a package of Juicy Fruit back in Pennsylvania, but he and Becky had shared it out before they reached the Ohio border. Juicy Fruit was a waste of money. That citrus flash of sugar was always gone in four chews and—he felt a stiff paper flap and withdrew a book of matches. Cal did not smoke, but they had been giving them away free at the little liquor store across the street from the Kaskaskia Dragon in Vandalia. It had a picture of the thirty-five-foot-long stainless-steel dragon on the cover. Becky and Cal had paid for a fistful of tokens, and spent most of the early evening feeding the big metal dragon to watch jets of burning propane erupt from its nostrils. Cal imagined the dragon set down in the field, and went dizzy with pleasure at the thought of it exhaling a destroying plume of fire into the grass.

He turned the matchbook over in his hand, thumbing soft cardboard.

Burn the field, he thought. Burn the fucking field. The tall grass would go the way of all straw when fed to flame.

He visualized a river of burning grass, sparks and shreds of toasted weed drifting into the air. It was such a strong mental image, he could close his eyes and almost smell it, the somehow wholesome late-summer reek of burning green.

And what if the flames turned back on him? What if it caught Becky out there somewhere? What if she was passed out, and woke to the stink of her own burning hair?

No. Becky would stay ahead of it. He would stay ahead of it. The idea was in him that he had to hurt the grass, show it he wasn't taking any more shit, and then it would let him—let them both—go. Every time a strand of grass brushed his cheek, he felt it was teasing him, having fun with him.

He rose on sore legs, and yanked at the grass. It was tough old rope, tough and sharp, and it hurt his hands, but he wrenched some loose, and crushed it into a pile and knelt before it, a penitent at a private altar. He tore a match loose, put it against the strike strip, folded the cover against it to hold it in place, and yanked. Fire spurted. His face was close and he inhaled a burning whiff of sulfur.

The match went out the moment he touched it to the wet grass, the stems heavy with a dew that never dried, and dense with juice.

His hand shook when he lit the next.

It hissed as he touched it to the grass and it went out. Hadn't Jack London written a story about this?

Another. Another. Each match made a fat little puff of smoke as soon as it touched the wet green. One didn't even make it into the grass, but was huffed out by the gentle breeze as soon as it was lit.

Finally, when there were six matches left, he lit one, and then, in desperation, touched it to the book itself. The paper matchbook ignited in a hot white flash and he dropped it into the nest of singed but still damp grass. For a moment it settled in the top of this mass of yellow-green weeds, a long, bright tongue of flame rising up from it.

Then the matchbook burned a hole in the damp grass and fell into the muck and went out.

He kicked at the whole mess in a spasm of sick, ugly despair. It was the only way to keep from crying again.

Then he sat still, eyes shut, forehead against his knee. He was tired and wanted to rest, wanted to lie on his back and watch the stars appear. At the same time, he did not want to lower himself into the clinging muck, didn't want it in his hair, soaking the back of his shirt. He was filthy enough as it was. His bare legs were striped from the flogging the sharp edges of the grass had given him. He thought he should try walking toward the road again—before the light was completely gone—but could hardly bear to stand.

What caused him to rise at last was the faraway sound of a car alarm going off. But not just any car alarm, no. This one didn't go wah-wah-wah, like most of them; this one went WHEEK-honk, WHEEK-honk, WHEEK-honk. So far as he knew, only old Mazdas wheek-honked like that when they were violated, flashing their headlights in time.

Like the one in which he and Becky had set out to cross the country.
WHEEK-honk, WHEEK-honk, WHEEK-honk.

His legs were tired, but he jumped up anyway. The road was closer again (not that it mattered), and yes, he could see a pair of flashing headlights. Not much else, but he didn't need to see much else to guess what was going on. The people along this stretch of the highway would know all about the field of tall grass across from the church and the defunct bowling alley. They would know to keep their own children on the safe side of the road. And when the occasional tourist heard cries for help and disappeared into the tall grass, determined to do the Good Samaritan bit, the locals visited the cars and took whatever there was worth taking.

They probably love this old field. And fear it. And worship it. And—

He tried to shut off the logical conclusion but couldn't.

And sacrifice to it. The swag they find in the trunks and glove compartments? Just a little bonus.

He wanted Becky. Oh God, how he wanted Becky. And oh God, how he wanted something to eat. He couldn't decide which he wanted more.

"Becky? Becky?"

Nothing. Overhead, stars were now glimmering.

Cal dropped to his knees, pressed his hands into the mucky ground, and dredged up more water. He drank it, trying to filter the grit with his teeth. *If Becky was with me, we could figure this out. I know we could. Because Ike and Mike, they think alike.*

He got more water, this time forgetting to filter it and swallowing more grit. Also something that wriggled. A bug, or maybe a small worm. Well, so what? It was protein, right?

"I'll never find her," Cal said. He stared at the darkening, waving grass. "Because you won't let me, will you? You keep the people who love each other apart, don't you? That's Job One, right? We'll just circle around and around, calling to each other, until we go insane."

Except Becky had stopped calling. Like Mom, Becky had gone dar—

"It doesn't have to be that way," a small clear voice said.

Cal's head jerked around. A little boy in mud-spattered clothes was standing there. His face was pinched and filthy. In one hand he held a dead crow by one yellow leg.

"Tobin?" Cal whispered.

"That's me." The boy raised the crow to his mouth and buried his face in its belly. Feathers crackled. The crow nodded its dead head as if to say *That's right, get right in there, get to the meat of the thing.*

Cal would have said he was too tired to spring after his latest jump, but horror has its own imperatives, and he sprang anyway. He tore the crow out of the boy's muddy hands, barely registering the guts unraveling from its open belly. Although he did see the feather stuck to the side of the boy's mouth. He saw that very well, even in the gathering gloom.

"You can't eat that! Jesus, kid! What are you, crazy?"

"Not crazy, Captain Cal, just hungry. And the crows aren't bad. I couldn't eat any of Freddy. I loved him, see. Dad ate some, but I didn't. Course, I hadn't touched the rock then. When you touch the rock—hug it, like—you can see. You just know a lot more. It makes you hungrier, though. And like my dad says, a man's meat and a man's gotta eat. After we went to the rock we separated, but he said we could find each other again anytime we wanted."

Cal was still one turn back. "Freddy?"

"He was our golden. Did great Frisbee catches. Just like a dog on TV. It's easier to find things in here once they're dead. The field doesn't move dead things around." His eyes gleamed in the fading light, and he looked at the mangled crow, which Cal was still holding. "I think most birds steer clear of the grass. I think they know, and tell each other. But some don't listen. Crows don't listen the most, I guess, because there are quite a few dead ones in here. Wander around for a while and you find them."

Cal said, "Tobin, did you lure us in here? Tell me. I won't be mad. Your father made you do it, I bet."

"We heard someone yelling. A little girl. She said she was lost. That's how we got in. That's how it works." He paused. "My dad killed your sister, I bet."

"How do you know she's my sister?"

"The rock," he said simply. "The rock teaches you to hear the grass, and the tall grass knows everything."

"Then you must know if she's dead or not."

"I could find out for you," Tobin said. "No. I can do better than that. I can show you. Do you want to go see? Do you want to check on her? Come on. Follow me."

Without waiting for a reply, the kid turned and walked into the grass. Cal dropped the dead crow and bolted after him, not wanting to lose sight of him even for a second. If he did, he might wander around forever without finding him again. I won't be mad, he'd told Tobin, but he was mad. Really mad. Not mad enough to kill a kid, of course not (probably of course not), but he wasn't going to let the little Judas-goat out of his sight, either.

Only he did, because the moon rose above the grass, bloated and orange. It looks pregnant, he thought, and when he looked back down, Tobin was gone. He forced his tired legs to run, shoving through the grass, filling his lungs to call. Then there was no more grass to shove. He was in a clearing—a real clearing, not just beaten-down grass. In the middle of it, a huge black rock jutted out of the ground. It was the size of a pickup truck and inscribed all over with tiny dancing stick men. They were white, and seemed to float. They seemed to move.

Tobin stood beside it, then put out one hand and touched it. He shivered—not in fear, Cal thought, but in pleasure. "Boy, that feels good. Come on, Captain Cal. Try it." He beckoned.

Cal walked toward the rock.

• • •

There was a car alarm for a bit, then it stopped. The sound went in Becky's ears but made no connection to her brain. She crawled. She did it without thinking. Each time a fresh cramp struck her, she stopped with her forehead pressed against the muck and her bottom in the air, like one of the faithful saluting Allah. When the cramp passed, she crawled some more. Her mud-smeared hair was stuck to her face. Her legs were wet with whatever was running out of her. She felt it running out of her but didn't think about it any more than she had thought about the car alarm. She licked water off the grass as she crawled, turning her head this way and that, flicking her tongue like a snake, snoop-sloop. She did it without thinking.

The moon came up, huge and orange. She twisted her head to look at it and when she did, the worst cramp yet hit her. This one didn't pass. She flopped over on her back and clawed her shorts and panties down. Both were soaked dark. At last a clear and coherent thought came, forking through her mind like a stroke of heat lightning: The baby!

She lay on her back in the grass with her bloody clothes around her ankles and her knees spread and her hands in her crotch. Snotty stuff squelched through her fingers. Then came a paralyzing cramp, and with it something round and hard. A skull. Its curve fit her hands with sweet perfection. It was Justine (if a girl), or Brady (if a boy). She had been lying to all of them about not having made up her mind; she had known from the first that this baby was going to be a keeper.

She tried to shriek and nothing came out but a whispery hhhhaaaahhh sound. The moon peered at her, a bloodshot dragon's eye. She pushed as hard as she could, her belly like a board, her ass screwed down into the mucky ground. Something tore. Something slid. Something arrived in her hands. Suddenly she was empty down there, so empty, but at least her hands were full.

Into the red-orange moonlight she raised the child of her body, thinking, It's all right, women all over the world give birth in fields.

It was Justine.

"Hey, baby girl," she croaked. "Oooh, you're so small."

And so silent.

. . .

Close up, it was easy to see the rock wasn't from Kansas. It had the black glassy quality of volcanic stone. The moonlight cast an iridescent sheen on its angled surfaces, creating slicks of light in tones of jade and pearl.

The stick men and the stick women held hands as they danced into curving waves of grass.

From eight steps back, they seemed to float just slightly above the surface of that great chunk of what-was-probably-not-obsidian.

From six steps back, they seemed to hang suspended just beneath the black glassy surface, objects sculpted from light, hologramlike. It was impossible to keep them in focus. It was impossible to look away.

Four steps away from the rock, he could hear it. The rock emitted a discreet buzz, like the electrified filament in a tungsten lamp. He could not feel it, however—he was not aware of the left side of his face beginning to pink, as if from sunburn. He had no sensation of heat at all.

Get away from it, he thought, but found it curiously difficult to step backward. His feet didn't seem to move in that direction anymore.

"I thought you were going to take me to Becky."

"I said we were going to check on her. We are. We'll check with the stone."

"I don't care about your goddamn—I just want Becky."

"If you touch the rock you won't be lost anymore," Tobin said. "You won't ever be lost again. You'll be redeemed. Isn't that nice?" He absentmindedly removed the black feather that had been stuck to the corner of his mouth.

"No," Cal said. "I don't think it is. I'd rather stay lost." Maybe it was just his imagination, but the buzzing seemed to be getting louder.

"No one would rather stay lost," the boy said, amiably. "Becky doesn't want to stay lost. She miscarried. If you can't find her, I think she'll probably die."

"You're lying," he said, without any conviction.

He might've inched a half step closer. A soft, fascinating light had begun to rise in the center of the rock, behind those floating stick figures . . . as if that buzzing tungsten he could hear was embedded about two feet beneath the surface of the stone, and someone was slowly dialing it up.

"I'm not," the boy said. "Look close, and you can see her."

Down in the smoked-quartz interior of the rock, he saw the dim lines of a human face. He thought, at first, he was looking at his own reflection. But although it was similar, it wasn't his. It was Becky, her lips peeled back in a doglike grimace of pain. Clots of filth smeared one side of her face. Tendons strained in her throat.

"Beck?" he said, as if she might be able to hear him.

He took another step forward—he couldn't help himself—leaning in to see. His palms were raised before him, in a kind of go-no-further gesture, but he could not feel them beginning to blister from whatever was radiating from the stone.

No, too close, he thought, and tried to fling himself backward, but couldn't get traction. Instead, his heels slid, as if he stood at the top of a mound of soft earth giving way beneath him. But the ground was flat; he slid forward because the stone had him, it had its own gravity, and it drew him as a magnet draws iron scrap.

Deep in the vast, jagged crystal ball of the great rock, Becky opened her eyes, and seemed to stare at him in wonder and terror.

The buzzing rose in his head.

The wind rose with it. The grass flung itself from side to side, ecstatically.

In the last instant, he became aware that his flesh was burning, that his skin was boiling in the unnatural climate that existed in the immediate space right around the rock. He knew when he touched the stone, it would be like setting his palms on a heated frying pan, and he began to scream—

—then stopped, the sound catching in his suddenly constricted throat.

The stone wasn't hot at all. It was cool. It was blessedly cool and he laid his face upon it, a weary pilgrim who has finally arrived at his destination, and can rest at last.

• • •

When Becky lifted her head, the sun was either coming up or going down, and her stomach hurt, as if she were recovering from a week of stomach flu. She wiped the sweat off her face with the back of one arm, pushed herself to her feet, and walked out of the grass, straight to the car. She was relieved to discover the keys were still hanging from the ignition. Becky pulled out of the lot and eased on up the road, driving at a leisurely pace.

At first she didn't know where she was going. It was hard to think past the pain in her abdomen, which came in waves. Sometimes it was a dull throb, the soreness of overworked muscles; other times it would intensify without warning into a sharp, somehow watery pain that lanced her through the bowels, and burned in her crotch. Her face was hot and feverish and even driving with the windows down didn't cool her off.

Now it was coming on for night and the dying day smelled of fresh-mown lawns and backyard barbecues and girls getting ready to go out on dates and baseball under the lights. She rolled through the streets of Durham, New Hampshire, in the dull red glow, the sun a bloated drop of blood on the horizon. She sailed past Stratham Hill Park, where she had run with her track team in high school. She took a turn around the baseball field. An aluminum bat chinked. Boys shouted. A dark figure sprinted for first base with his head down.

Becky drove distracted, chanting one of her limericks to herself, only half-aware she was doing it. She whisper-sang the oldest one she had been able to find when she was researching her paper, a limerick that had been written well before the form devolved into grotty riffs on fucking, although it pointed in that direction:

"A girl once hid in tall grass," she crooned.
"And ambushed any boy who walked past.
As lions eat gazelles,

>   so many men fell,
> and each tasted better than the last."

A girl, she thought, almost randomly. Her girl. It came to her, then, what she was doing. She was out looking for her girl, the one she was supposed to be babysitting, and oh Jesus what an unholy fucking mess, the kid had wandered off on her, and Becky had to find her before the parents got home, and it was getting dark fast, and she couldn't even remember the little shit's name.

She struggled to remember how this could've happened. For a moment the recent past was a maddening blank. Then it came to her. The girl wanted to swing in the backyard, and Becky said Go on, that's fine, hardly paying any attention. At the time she was text-messaging with Travis McKean. They were having a fight. Becky didn't even hear the back screen door slapping shut.

what am i supposed to tell my mom, Travis said, i don't even know if I want to stay in college let alone start a family. And this gem: if we get married will i have to say I DO to your bro too? hes always around sitting on your bed reading skateboreding magazine, i m amazed he wasn't sitting there watching the night i got you pregnant. You want a family you should start one with him

She had made a little scream down in her throat and chucked the phone against the wall, leaving a dent in the plaster, hoped the parents came back drunk and didn't notice. (Who were the parents, anyway? Whose house was this?) Beck had wandered to the picture window that looked into the backyard, pushing her hair away from her face, trying to get her calm back—and saw the empty swing moving gently in the breeze, chains softly squalling. The back gate was open to the driveway.

She went out into the jasmine-scented evening and shouted. She shouted in the driveway. She shouted in the yard. She shouted until her stomach hurt. She stood in the center of the empty road and yelled "Hey, kid, hey!" with her hands cupped around her mouth. She walked down the block and into the grass and spent what felt like days pushing through the high weeds, looking for the wayward child, her lost responsibility. When she emerged at last, the car was waiting for her, and she took off. And here she was, driving aimlessly, scanning the sidewalks, a desperate, animal panic rising inside her. She had lost her girl. Her girl had gotten away from her—wayward child, lost responsibility—and who knew what would happen to her, what might be happening to her right now. The not-knowing made her stomach hurt. It made her stomach hurt bad.

A storm of little birds flowed through the darkness above the road.

Her throat was dry. She was so fucking thirsty she could hardly stand it.

Pain knifed her, went in and out, like a lover.

When she drove past the baseball field for a second time, the players had all gone home. Game called on account of darkness, she thought, a phrase which caused her arms to prickle with goosebumps, and that was when she heard a child shout.

"BECKY!" shouted the little girl. "IT'S TIME TO EAT!" As if Becky were the one who was lost. "IT'S TIME TO COME EAT!"

"WHAT ARE YOU DOING, LITTLE GIRL?" Becky screamed back, pulling over to the curb. "YOU COME HERE! YOU COME HERE RIGHT NOW!"

"YOU'LL HAVE TO FIIIND ME!" screamed the girl, her voice giddy with delight. "FOLLOW MY VOICE!"

The shouts seemed to be coming from the far side of the field, where the grass was high. Hadn't she already looked there? Hadn't she tramped all through the grass, trying to find her? Hadn't she gotten a little lost in the grass herself?

"THERE WAS AN OLD FARMER FROM LEEDS!" the girl shouted.

Becky started across the infield. She took two steps and there was a tearing sensation in her womb and she cried out.

"WHO SWALLOWED A BAG FULLA SEEDS!" the girl trilled, her voice vibrating with barely controlled laughter.

Becky stopped, exhaled the pain, and when the worst of it had passed, she took another cautious step. Immediately, the pain returned, worse than before. She had a sensation of things shearing inside, as if her intestines were a bedsheet, stretched tight, beginning to rip down the middle.

"BIG BUNCHES OF GRASS," the girl yodeled, "SPROUTED OUT OF HIS ASS!"

Becky sobbed again, took a third staggering step, almost to second base now, the tall grass not far away, and then another bolt of pain ran her through and she dropped to her knees.

"AND HIS BALLS GREW ALL SHAGGY WITH WEEDS!"

the girl yelled, voice quivering with laughter.

Becky gripped the sagging, empty waterskin of her stomach and shut her eyes and lowered her head, and waited for relief, and when she felt the tiniest bit better, she opened her eyes . . .

• • •

And Cal was there, in the ashy light of dawn, looking down at her. His own eyes were sharp and avid.

"Don't try to move," he said. "Not for a while. Just rest. I'm here."

He was naked from the waist up, kneeling beside her. His scrawny chest was very pale in the dove-colored half-light. His face was sunburned—badly, a blister right on the end of his nose—but aside from that he looked rested and well. No, more than that: He looked bright-eyed and bushy-tailed.

"The baby," she tried to say, but nothing would come out, just a scraping click, the sound of someone trying to pick a rusty lock with rusty tools.

"Are you thirsty? Bet you are. Here. Take this. Put it in your mouth." He pushed a soaked, cold twist of his T-shirt into her mouth. He had saturated it with water and rolled it up into a rope.

She sucked at it avidly, an infant hungrily nursing.

"No," he said, "no more. You'll make yourself sick." Taking the wet cotton rope away from her, leaving her gasping like a fish in a pail.

"Baby," she whispered.

Cal grinned at her—his best, zaniest grin. "Isn't she great? I've got her. She's perfect. Out of the oven and baked just right!"

He reached to the side and lifted up a bundle wrapped in someone else's T-shirt. She saw a little snub of bluish nose protruding from the shroud. No; not a shroud. Shrouds were for dead bodies. It was swaddling. She had delivered a child here, out in the high grass, and hadn't even needed the shelter of a manger.

Cal, as always, spoke as if he had a direct line to her private thoughts. "Aren't you the little Mother Mary? Wonder when the Wise Men will show up! Wonder what gifts they'll have for us!"

A freckled, sunburnt boy appeared behind Cal. He was bare-chested too. It was probably his shirt wound around the baby. He bent over, hands on his knees, to look at her swaddled infant.

"Isn't she wonderful?" Cal asked, showing the boy.

"Scrumptious, Captain Cal," the boy said.

Becky closed her eyes.

• • •

She drove in the dusk, the window down, the breeze fanning her hair back from her face. The tall grass bordered both sides of the road, stretching ahead of her as far as she could see. She would be driving through it the rest of her life.

"A girl once hid in tall grass," she sang to herself. "And ambushed any boy who walked past."

The grass rustled and scratched at the sky.

• • •

She opened her eyes for a few moments, later in the morning.

Her brother was holding a doll's leg in one hand, filthy from the mud. He stared at her with a bright, stupid fascination, while he chewed on it. It was a lifelike thing, chubby and plump looking, but a little small, and also a funny pale-blue color, like almost frozen milk. Cal, you can't eat plastic, she thought of saying, but it was just too much work.

The little boy sat behind him, turned in profile, licking something off his palms. Strawberry jelly, it looked like.

There was a sharp smell in the air, an odor like a fresh-opened tin of fish. It made her stomach rumble. But she was too weak to sit up, too weak to say anything, and when she lowered her head against the ground and shut her eyes, she sank straight back into sleep.

• • •

This time there were no dreams.

Somewhere a dog barked: roop-roop. A hammer began to fall, one ringing whack after another, calling Becky back to consciousness.

Her lips were dry and cracked and she was thirsty once more. Thirsty and hungry. She felt as if she had been kicked in the stomach a few dozen times.

"Cal," she whispered. "Cal."

"You need to eat," he said, and put a string of something cold and salty in her mouth. His fingers had blood on them.

If she had been anywhere near in her right mind she might've gagged. But it tasted good, actually, a salty-sweet strand of something, with the fatty texture of a sardine. It even smelled a little like a sardine. She sucked at it much as she had sucked at the wet rope of Cal's shirt.

Cal hiccuped as she sucked the strand of whatever it was into her mouth, sucked it in like spaghetti and swallowed. It had a bad aftertaste, bitter-sour, but even that was sort of nice. Like the food equivalent of the taste you got after drinking a margarita and licking some of the salt off the rim of your glass. Cal's hiccup sounded almost like a sob of laughter.

"Give her another piece," said the little boy, leaning over Cal's shoulder.

Cal gave her another piece. "Yum yum. Snark that li'l baby right down."

She swallowed and shut her eyes again.

• • •

When she next found herself awake, she was over Cal's shoulder, and she was moving. Her head bobbed and her stomach heaved with each step.

She whispered: "Did we eat?"

"Yes."

"What did we eat?"

"Something scrumptious. Scrump-tiddly-umptious."

"Cal, what did we eat?"

He didn't answer, just pushed aside grass spattered with maroon droplets and walked into a clearing. In the center was a huge black rock. Standing beside it was the little kid.

There you are, she thought. I chased you all over the neighborhood.

Only that hadn't been a rock. You couldn't chase a rock. It had been a girl.

A girl. My girl. My responsi—

"WHAT DID WE EAT?" She began to pound him, but her fists were weak, weak. "OH GOD! OH MY JESUS!"

He set her down and looked at her first with surprise and then amusement. "What do you think we ate?" He looked at the boy, who was grinning and shaking his head, the way you do when someone's just pulled a really hilarious boner. "Beck . . . honey . . . we just ate some of the grass. Grass and seeds and so on. Cows do it all the time."

"There was an old farmer from Leeds," the boy sang, and put his hands to his mouth to stifle his giggles. His fingers were red. "He was hungry and had special needs."

"I don't believe you," Becky said, but her voice sounded faint. She was looking at the rock. It was incised all over with little dancing figures. And yes, in this early light they did seem to dance. To be moving around in rising spirals, like the stripes on a barber pole.

"Really, Beck. The baby is—is great. Safe. I'm already doing the uncle thing. Touch the rock, and you'll see. You'll understand. Touch the rock, and you'll be—"

He looked at the boy.

"Redeemed!" Tobin shouted, and they laughed together.

Ike and Mike, Becky thought. They laugh alike.

She walked toward it . . . put her hand out . . . then drew back. What she had eaten hadn't tasted like grass. It had tasted like sardines. Like the final sweet-salty-bitter swallow of a margarita. And like . . .

Like me. Like licking sweat from my own armpit. Or . . . or . . .

She began to shriek. She tried to turn away, but Cal had her by one flailing arm and Tobin by the other. She should have been able to break free from the child, at least, but she was still weak. And the rock. It was pulling at her, too.

"Touch it," Cal whispered. "You'll stop being sad. You'll see the baby is all right. Little Justine. She's better than all right. She's elemental. Becky—she flows."

"Yeah," Tobin said. "Touch the rock. You'll see. You won't be lost out here anymore. You'll understand the grass then. You'll be part of it. Like Justine is part of it."

They escorted her to the rock. It hummed busily. Happily. From inside there came the most wondrous glow. On the outside, tiny stick men and stick women danced with their stick hands held high. There was music. She thought: All flesh is grass.

Becky DeMuth hugged the rock.

• • •

There were seven of them in an old RV held together by spit, baling wire, and—perhaps—the resin of all the dope that had been smoked inside its rusty walls. Printed on one side, amid a riot of red-and-orange psychedelia, was the word FURTHER, in honor of the 1939 International Harvester school bus in which Ken Kesey's Merry Pranksters had visited Woodstock during the summer of 1969. Back then all but the two oldest of these latter-day hippies had yet to be born.

Just lately the twenty-first-century Pranksters had been in Cawker City, paying homage to the World's Largest Ball of Twine. Since leaving, they had busted mega-amounts of dope, and all of them were hungry.

It was Twista, the youngest of them, who spotted the Black Rock of the Redeemer, with its soaring white steeple and oh-so-convenient parking lot. "Church picnic!" he shouted from his seat beside Pa Cool, who was driving. Twista bounced up and down, the buckles on his bib overalls jingling. "Church picnic! Church picnic!"

The others took it up. Pa looked at Ma in the rearview. When she shrugged and nodded, he pulled FURTHER into the lot and parked beside a dusty Mazda with New Hampshire license plates.

The Pranksters (all wearing Ball of Twine souvenir T-shirts and all smelling of superbud) piled out. Pa and Ma, as the eldest, were the captain and first mate of the good ship FURTHER, and the other five—MaryKat, Jeepster, Eleanor Rigby, Frankie the Wiz, and Twista—were perfectly willing to follow orders, pulling out the barbecue, the cooler of meat, and—of course—the beer. Jeepster and the Wiz were just setting up the grill when they heard the first faint voice.

"Help! Help! Somebody help me!"

"That sounds like a woman," Eleanor said.

"Help! Somebody please! I'm lost!"

"That's not a woman," Twista said. "That's a little kid."

"Far out," MaryKat said. She was cataclysmically stoned, and it was all she could think to say.

Pa looked at Ma. Ma looked at Pa. They were pushing sixty now and had been together a long time—long enough to have couples' telepathy.

"Kid wandered into the grass," Ma Cool said.

"Mom heard him yelling and went after him," Pa Cool said.

"Maybe too short to see their way back to the road," Ma said. "And now—"

"—they're both lost," Pa finished.

"Jeez, that sucks," Jeepster said. "I got lost once. It was in a mall."

"Far out," MaryKat said.

"Help! Anybody!" That was the woman.

"Let's go get them," Pa said. "We'll bring 'em out and feed 'em up."

"Good idea," the Wiz said. "Human kindness, man. I'm all about the human fuckin' kindness."

Ma Cool hadn't owned a watch in years, but was good at telling time by the sun. She squinted at it now, measuring the distance between the reddening ball and the field of grass, which seemed to stretch to the horizon. I bet all of Kansas looked that way before the people came and spoiled it all, she thought.

"It is a good idea," she said. "It's going on for five thirty, and I bet they're really hungry. Who's going to stay and set up the barbecue?"

There were no volunteers. Everyone had the munchies, but none of them wanted to miss the mercy mission. In the end, all of them trooped across Route 400 and entered into the tall grass.

FURTHER.

CPSIA information can be obtained
at www.ICGtesting.com
Printed in the USA
LVHW050534090321
680926LV00002B/6

9 781732 970458